Fatima and the Juniper Tree

Fatima and the Juniper Tree

Jennifer Wortham, Dr.PH

Inspiration Pointe Press

Book Design and Illustrations by Kevin Barnard, San Francisco, CA
kevin@barnardgraphics.com

Published by Inspiration Pointe Press, Los Angeles, CA

First edition printed in the United States of America

ISBN: 978-0-9968406-5-1

Fatima and the Juniper Tree
is a fable inspired by real events
and is a modern adaptation of "The Juniper Tree,"
a German allegory published in Low German by the Brothers Grimm,
in *Grimms' Fairy Tales* in 1812 (Khm 47).

All proceeds from the sale of this book will support organizations dedicated to protecting the dignity of children throughout the world.

Trigger Warning: This book addresses child abuse. The theme of this story may be disturbing to some readers. Reading or hearing about a traumatic event can trigger a memory or emotional response related to a painful or frightening event they may have experienced in the past. Triggering events can lead to intense emotional and physical reactions, including anxiety, panic attacks, flashbacks, or other trauma-related symptoms. For this reason, many discussions, articles, or media that include potentially distressing content may come with a trigger warning to alert readers or viewers of the sensitive nature of the content.

This book is dedicated to the unsung heroes
who help make the magic happen each and every day.

Thank you for your service.

The great spirit that lives within the juniper tree,
lives in us all. If we open our hearts, it has the power
to bring us together to accomplish things that
no one person can accomplish on their own.

The Coop Harvard Square © Dominique Derenne

1

It was a crisp fall day as Jenny strode briskly through the heart of Cambridge, her footsteps echoing off the historic brick and cobblestone pathways of Harvard Square. The iconic spires of Harvard University loomed ahead, a reminder of the great privilege she received to conduct research with leading scholars from around the world, and the opportunity to fulfill a lifelong dream.

The crimson-tinged leaves of fall fluttered around her, mirroring the swirl of emotions inside: excitement, trepidation, and a deep reverence for the journey ahead. As she passed historic brownstone buildings and high-tech research facilities, Jenny felt both grounded in the present and tethered to the legacies of past scholars who had walked these paths before her. With its rich tapestry of history and innovation, Harvard was a magical place that held the promise of unlimited possibilities.

Earlier in the year, the world was struck with a deadly virus, referred to as COVID-19, resulting in an unprecedented global pandemic. In response, the University had transitioned to an all-virtual learning environment, and most of the shops, and cafés that were normally full of life were shuttered due to the city's mandatory quarantine. The few exceptions were pharmacies, take-out restaurants, convenience stores, and her destination, The Harvard Coop Bookstore.

Jenny had joined the research team at Harvard's Human Flourishing Program to gain a deeper understanding of the impact of religion and spirituality on health and wellbeing. She journeyed to the bookstore to pick up a few books on spirituality to inspire her research. Much of the information she needed could be found online, but she had grown restless of being cooped up indoors, and the bookstore provided a much needed reprieve from the months of isolation.

As she walked into the historic building, the scent of books and polished wood enveloped her, immediately transporting her to a world where knowledge and discovery melded into one. The store, with its high ceilings, mahogany shelves, and creaky wooden floors, whispered tales of countless researchers, scholars, and curious minds who had walked its aisles over the past century.

She spent hours perusing the shelves of the quiet store, letting her fingers dance over the spines of books, each one a repository of knowledge and insight. Every now and then, she'd pull out a volume, captivated by its title or the brief synopsis on the back cover, and would lose herself in its pages, often sitting on the floor, surrounded by a growing pile of chosen treasures.

To her delight, she stumbled upon an old book filled with folklore and fairy tales that reminded her of her childhood. The pages of the book had vivid pictures of curious creatures, known as Wesens, and monsters, villains, handsome princes, and magical beings in faraway kingdoms. She smiled as she recognized the characters of the beloved bedtime stories her mother read to her as a young girl.

Every story in the book had a unique cast of characters, yet all shared a common thread of the human experience. The characters faced challenges that echoed across time—struggles for identity, battles against injustice, and quests for personal growth. As she delved deeper into the book, Jenny realized that the adversities and triumphs faced by the characters of the past were not too dissimilar from those many around the world are experiencing today.

The bookstore was closing, and Jenny was only halfway through the book, so she made a snap decision to buy it along with several books on spirituality. She paid for the books, put them into her backpack, and headed home.

2

WALKING DOWN THE COBBLESTONE PATH to her brownstone, Jenny reflected on the stories in the book of folklore tucked in her backpack. She pondered on the twists and turns that life took, the unexpected connections that formed, and the intricate interplay of fate and choice that shaped our destinies.

The tales in the book spanned cultures and epochs, each with its own take on the human experience and the mysteries of existence. Some stories spoke of heroes destined for greatness, their paths illuminated by stars and prophecies. Others told of ordinary souls who, by sheer will and choice, altered the course of their lives and impacted those around them in profound ways.

As she turned the corner to her block, Jenny saw a group of teenage boys playing football on the field across the street. The boys wore masks as they played, a stark reminder of the global COVID pandemic that had resurged in recent months. They seemed oblivious to the threats that had gripped the world, as they laughed, shouted, and kicked the ball with fervor, capturing the indomitable spirit of youth that thrived even in the face of adversity.

Jenny stopped and watched the boys for a few minutes, smiling as she thought of her brothers and their friends playing ball when they were young boys. Despite the masks and the intermittent reminders to maintain distance, the essence of the game remained unchanged – camaraderie, competition, and sheer fun. It was heartwarming and bittersweet, a semblance of life as it once was, and the promise of life returning to normal.

As she continued down the sidewalk, Jenny passed by a quaint cottage with a white picket fence, and she noticed a dog sleeping peacefully on the porch. When the dog sensed her presence, it awoke and began barking. Its piercing howl echoed through the quiet street, reverberating off the cobblestones. Then one by one, sensing a threat, other dogs nearby began barking in unison, standing their ground and growling ferociously as they protected their turf. The once serene street now felt like a corridor of alarm, every corner echoing with the sounds of canines declaring their dominion.

Jenny's heart skipped a beat, and the grip of fear and panic tightened around her chest as sudden waves of the memories of the night she lost her dignity to a group of boys crashed into her consciousness with an intensity that took her breath away. She halted, frozen in place as a flood of sensations made her feel she was reliving that moment again. Jenny's brain seemed to be fighting against an invisible force that was pushing her toward the edge of an abyss. She struggled to catch her breath, time slowed, and everything blurred.

One by one, the dogs ceased their barking and shifted their focus to other things around them. It was as if they shared an understanding that whatever had initially triggered their response was no longer a cause for concern. They returned to their resting spots in yards or on porches, curling up into comfortable positions. As the last echoes of barking faded into the background, the neighborhood settled back into its usual peaceful ambiance. Only the rustling leaves and distant sounds of the children playing in the park remained.

After a few minutes, Jenny's thoughts returned to the present. She knew there was no danger, but her heart was still racing as the surge of adrenaline continued to course through her veins. Her legs felt heavy, her hands were shaking, she grew nauseous, and faint. She had experienced panic attacks before, but never as intensely as the one that gripped her that day.

Emotionally exhausted and drained of all her energy, Jenny sat on a small patch of grass beneath a great juniper tree to catch her breath. She rested her back against the trunk of the tree and waited for her heartrate to slow. The scent of pine and sweet evergreen enveloped her like a gentle embrace, connecting her to the tree's enduring spirit and calming her jittery nerves. With each breath she took, Jenny felt a sense of grounding, as if the scent of juniper were anchoring her to the present moment.

In the distance, Jenny heard a bird singing, calming her like a lullaby. Her heartbeat slowly returned to normal, and the awareness of her surroundings returned. Then, a soft breeze grazed the leaves in the trees, as though it was whispering an ancient chant of peace. It was a moment of pure serenity, a connection to something greater than herself – a reminder that there was a refuge from the world's chaos in the embrace of nature. She closed her eyes and drifted to sleep.

3

Jenny's peaceful slumber was interrupted by a gentle rustling of the leaves in the branches above. She looked about and saw a beautiful bird emerge from within the great tree. She had never seen such a bird; its feathers were pink and white, and it had black eyes and a golden beak.

To Jenny's amazement, the bird spoke to her with a soft, melodic voice. "Hello, what is your name?" the bird asked as it fluttered about. "My name is Jenny; what is your name?" "My name is Fatima," said the bird. "Where did you come from?" asked Jenny. "I come from a faraway place called Freetown, by the sea in Sierra Leone," Fatima said as she flew down to perch on a rock nearby.

Fatima tucked her wings, and with concern in her voice, she added, "I sense a deep pain in your heart, Jenny. Would you like to tell me what happened to cause you such grief?" Jenny nodded and told Fatima of the night she lost her dignity to a group of boys who had entered her room through her window when she was a young girl. It was the first time she felt comfortable sharing her story.

As the emotions Jenny had buried for years surged to the surface, tears welled in her eyes, and a lump formed in her throat. Each tear seemed to carry with it a piece of the pain she had kept hidden away, locked in a secret chamber of her heart. It was as if the act of speaking about the event gave voice to her inner anguish, validating the trauma she had kept hidden for so long.

Fatima listened with compassion to all that Jenny shared. "It took great courage for you to share your story, Jenny. I understand your suffering, for I once faced a similar fate." "What did you do?" asked Jenny.

"I shared my burden with one of the women in my village, and she helped me. Years later, I told my husband what had happened, and he created policies that led to new laws to help protect the children in my country from those who might harm them."

"I think we should encourage all countries to implement such laws, so all the children of the world can be safe," said Jenny. "Perhaps we could establish a world day to raise awareness and support."

"That is a fabulous idea, Jenny." said Fatima.

Just then, the bell in the church tower rang five times, and Fatima realized it was time for her to return home. "I must fly home now, Jenny. Meet me here tomorrow, before the sun sets, and you can share your idea with my husband. I believe he can help find a way to encourage the world's leaders to join us in protecting children's dignity." said Fatima.

Then she spread her great wings and took flight, singing a beautiful song where love formed an unbreakable shield to protect all the children of the world, and empathy served as a healing balm for those who were suffering.

Jenny climbed high into the great juniper tree and listened to Fatima's song as her new friend soared across the sky and vanished over the horizon. The sun had set, and Jenny shivered as a chill came into the air. She climbed down the tree, picked up her backpack, and walked home, thinking of Fatima's song with great hope, feeling her sorrows lifting with each step.

That night Jenny slept peacefully for the first time since she had been hurt so long ago, knowing in her heart that Fatima would keep her word.

4

THE NEXT MORNING, Jenny awoke refreshed and ready to face the day. She ate breakfast and got to work on her computer. She tried to pay attention to her research, but she could see the juniper tree from the window in her study, and she grew more restless as the hours went by. Finally, the clock struck 5 p.m., so Jenny gathered her things, tied her hair with a blue ribbon, ran down the steps, skipped down the street, and stood by the juniper tree, waiting patiently for her new friend.

A few moments later, a beautiful lady appeared in a flowing white gown. Her hair was wrapped in a white headscarf embroidered with gold trim. She wore a long scarf around her neck, and she had golden bangles on her wrists that glimmered in the light. Jenny stared in wonder, not sure what to say to the fine lady who appeared before her.

"Hello, Jenny, how are you today?" asked the lady.

Jenny was amazed as she recognized the voice; it was Fatima. How could it be, she wondered as she responded, "I am feeling much better today."

Fatima smiled and said, "That makes me ever so happy."

Jenny pulled the ribbon from her hair. "I brought you a gift," she said as she handed the ribbon to her friend.

"Thank you," said Fatima as she took a pin from beneath her headscarf and attached the ribbon to her dress. "It is a beautiful ribbon; I shall wear it always to remind me of our special mission," she said as she winked. Jenny beamed with happiness; glad the humble gift had pleased her friend. "I believe it is time for you to meet my husband, Julius. Are you ready?" asked Fatima.

Jenny nodded, "I am ready, but I'm a bit nervous." Fatima assured Jenny that all would be well, then she pulled a magic wand from her sleeve and reached out and touched the branch of the juniper tree three times. With each movement of her hand, the bangles she wore clinked together louder and louder. On the third tap of the wand, the great tree creaked and groaned, then it yawned and took a deep breath as though it was waking from a long nap.

Suddenly there was a brilliant flash of light, brighter than the lightning in the sky on a stormy night. Jenny shielded her eyes with her hands, and for a moment, she was afraid. Jenny peeked through her fingers when all grew quiet, and she could hardly believe her eyes. In place of the juniper tree stood a man with gold-rimmed spectacles wearing a green kaftan and a matching cap that shined like emeralds. Mesmerized by the energy that emanated from the great man, Jenny was quite speechless. She looked about for Fatima, but her friend had disappeared.

The man cleared his throat to get Jenny's attention, and in a kind voice, he said, "Hello, Ms. Jenny, my name is Julius."

Remembering her manners, Jenny bowed and said, "I am most honored to meet you."

Julius put his hands together, and he grew serious. "Fatima told me of your story, and I thought perhaps we might discuss your idea for establishing programs to protect the dignity of the world's children."

Julius began escorting Jenny home. As they walked, she shared her dreams of establishing an annual day of observance to raise awareness of the need to protect all children and help survivors of abuse reclaim their lives.

Julius listened to Jenny carefully as she spoke. "Your ideas are quite inspiring. I will talk with my advisors, and we shall consider your plan. I will send you a message when we have decided on the best path forward," said Julius. Knowing their meeting was ending, Jenny thanked Julius for taking the time to speak with her. When they arrived at her brownstone, a limousine with green and yellow flags was parked across the street.

As Julius and Jenny approached her building, an official-looking man in a black suit came about and stood by the car's back door. Julius reached out, took Jenny's hand in his warm embrace, and said, "It was a pleasure meeting you, Jenny."

"It was a pleasure meeting you as well, Julius. Please give my regards to Fatima," she added. Then Julius and the man in the smart suit got into the car, and she watched as it drove away.

That night as she drifted off to sleep, Jenny wondered if she might ever see Fatima again. Then, in her dreams, she saw her friend gliding gracefully over the land, watching over the children of the world, singing her song of love and compassion, reminding Jenny that the magic of their meeting would always remain alive in her heart.

5

A FEW WEEKS AFTER SHE MET JULIUS, there was a letter addressed to Jenny in the mailbox. She opened the letter, and a beautiful white feather fell from the envelope into her hand. The top of the letter had an official seal with a shield and two lions, and Jenny cried tears of joy when she read the words on the fine parchment paper.

"Dear Ms. Jenny, President Julius Maada Wonie Bio has assigned me an important task to help protect the world's children. I am to collaborate with my colleagues in the United Nations to implement a zero-tolerance policy against the abuse of child dignity. We would be most honored if you would come to the Mission in New York City during your summer break to meet with my staff and assist with executing this plan. Sincerely, His Excellency, Ambassador Alhaji Fanday Turay, Permanent Representative of the Republic of Sierra Leone to the United Nations."

Jenny felt a renewed sense of hope that she might be able to do something to help prevent children from being hurt as she had been when she was a young girl. She wrote to the Ambassador straightaway and accepted his invitation. In her letter, she vowed to do everything in her power to help him achieve his Mission.

Over the next few months, Jenny worked hard to finish her research project. With each day, her determination to establish a world day for children grew. It was time for the world's leaders to unite and take a stand to protect the dignity of children. With the support of President Bio and the First Lady, Jenny knew in her heart that anything was possible.

The time had finally arrived for Jenny to leave for New York to begin her new project. The anticipation bubbled within her, a mix of excitement and nervousness. This project wasn't just any ordinary project; it was the beginning of a movement, and its success could help change the lives of many around the globe.

Jenny boarded the train from Boston to New York and watched as the world whizzed by, a blur of cities, towns, and open countryside. She leaned her head against the window, feeling the gentle vibrations of the wheels as they rode the tracks beneath her feet. Her body rocked in unison with the gentle sway of the train, cradling her worries and thoughts and reminding her that sometimes, it is in the journey itself that we find the most profound moments of reflection and solace.

A few hours later, the train pulled into New York City's Penn Station. Jenny exited the train with her bag, and stepped onto the platform and inhaled the crisp air. As she walked into the main part of the station, there was a surge of energy and excitement as crowds of people dressed in vibrant colors and speaking foreign languages hurried past her in different directions.

She exited the station, where she saw towering skyscrapers reaching for the sky, their reflective surfaces capturing slivers of sunlight, casting a dazzling display across the cityscape. The pulsating rhythm of urban life, the immense buildings, and throngs of people seemed bigger than life. With her backpack slung over her shoulder, Jenny navigated through the crowd, her eyes wide open with wonder as she took in the sensory overload that surrounded her.

As she made her way through the bustling streets, Jenny could not help but marvel at the harmonious chaos of it all. The scents of street food mingled with exhaust fumes, creating a unique urban aroma. Neon signs and billboards painted the scene with a kaleidoscope of colors, each promising its brand of excitement. Street vendors peddled their wares, their voices rising above the cacophony of honking horns and animated conversations. It was an impressive sight to behold.

After walking several blocks, Jenny found herself at the rebuilt World Trade Center, surrounded by the grandeur of architectural marvels that seemed to stretch endlessly toward the heavens. Glass and steel structures coexisted with historic buildings, and a monument was etched into the landscape that honored the past World Trade Center and the many lives lost there in 2001, while embracing the future.

Jenny paused to take it all in, feeling a deep sense of humility, and awe. She had a momentary sense of anxiety, wondering how she might possibly learn how to navigate the complex city.

As the day turned into evening, the city's lights illuminated the skyline, casting a warm glow that seemed to embrace everyone within its reach. Jenny's initial apprehension had transformed into a bubbling excitement. She was ready to embrace the challenges, the vibrancy, and the transformative experiences that awaited her. The city's energy mirrored her own; together, they stood on the threshold of endless possibilities. The adventure was beginning.

6

THE FOLLOWING DAY Jenny stepped out of a taxi across from the United Nations headquarters. Atop tall poles, the flags of the one hundred and ninety-three nations fluttered in the breeze, forming a colorful corridor along the boulevard. She gazed up at the impressive sight with resolve, confident that they would find a way to get the leaders of the nations represented by the flags to support the world day for children.

Jenny walked a few short blocks to the Uganda House, where the Mission of Sierra Leone was housed. She was greeted warmly by a security guard who noted her name and called the receptionist at the Mission to alert them that she had arrived. Another guard escorted her to the elevator and took her to a suite on the sixth floor. The doors opened, and Jenny was greeted by Ambassador Sulimani, and Ms. Finda Sensi, the Ambassador's attaché. They sat in a large conference room, and more staff from the Mission arrived, each radiating an air of dedication and purpose.

As they exchanged warm greetings, Jenny felt a sense of belonging in this gathering of like-minded individuals who were determined to make a difference in the lives of the world's children. She listened to each person as they spoke passionately about the problem of the abuse of child dignity in Africa.

As they talked about the importance of education, awareness campaigns, and collaboration, Jenny's perspective as a survivor of abuse added a personal dimension to their efforts, reminding everyone of the impact they were striving to achieve.

Together, they made a grand plan to create a resolution to be passed by the entire UN. There was much to do, and they realized they would need help. Jenny called upon her colleagues Tyler, Matt, and Brendan at Harvard, and they agreed to provide technical support. Ambassador Sulimani, Ms. Finda, and Jenny visited Archbishop Caccia at the Mission of the Holy See. He spoke with the Secretariat of the Vatican, and the Secretariat talked to the Holy Father, and he agreed to support the resolution.

Next, Ambassador Turay called upon His Excellency Ambassador Tijjani-Muhammad-Bande, the Permanent Representative of the great nation of the Federal Republic of Nigeria to the United Nations, and his attaché Mr. Nnamdi Okechukwu Nze, to ask for their support. They called the Capital and spoke to their President, His Excellency Bola Tinubu, and he agreed that Nigeria could co-facilitate the resolution with Sierra Leone.

Then they launched a global campaign to gather support for the resolution, and other survivors who had found their voices joined the movement. Jenny saw firsthand the immense impact that the opportunity for survivors to transform their adversity into action had on their lives. It gave their suffering meaning and purpose and helped alleviate the sense of powerlessness they once experienced. The shared mission of establishing a world day bound all of them together in a unique way and their strength in numbers grew into an unstoppable force.

Over the next few months, Jenny and her friends Mark, Mike, Sara, Suzie, and others in the survivor community worked with Ms. Finda, Nnamdi, and the leadership of the United Nations Children's Fund and the Office of the Special Representative of the Secretary-General on Violence Against Children, to draft the language for the resolution.

Through long hours of planning, drafting documents, and attending meetings, Jenny saw the intricate web of international diplomacy and advocacy in action. And amidst the work, there were moments of connection that touched her deeply. As the months passed, Jenny's admiration for all those who worked at the United Nations grew. Their dedication, resilience, and unwavering commitment to making the world a better place for children was a true inspiration.

In September, the resolution was ready for presentation to the United Nations Social, Humanitarian, and Cultural Committee, known as the Third Committee. This crucial step included an in-depth review and discussion of the proposed language in the resolution until everyone approved and could advocate for support of the document to their leaders.

As the days progressed, the excitement of all involved mounted, and then the time finally arrived for the resolution to progress to the pivotal stage: presentation before the entire General Assembly. The Mission formally requested the placement of the resolution on the Assembly's calendar, and all waited in anticipation to learn when it might be scheduled, which they called "tabled."

A few days later, the office of the UN Secretary General relayed a message to the Mission. The resolution was scheduled to be presented during the Plenary session of the General Assembly, at a regular gathering of the member states set to convene on November 7, 2022. Jenny, brimming with excitement, eagerly shared this remarkable news not only with her colleagues at Harvard, but also with those in the survivor community who contributed to this remarkable achievement.

Amid the growing anticipation, Ambassador Turay received confirmation that H.E. Fatima Maada Bio, the First Lady of the Republic of Sierra Leone, would personally address the Assembly. This revelation ignited a spark of joy in Jenny, who was thrilled at the prospect of reuniting with her friend. With each passing day, the enthusiasm escalated as more and more nations expressed their commitment to sponsoring this momentous action.

As the appointed day drew near, their anticipation reached a crescendo. Hearts were filled with hope, and minds were alight with the possibilities that the resolution would hold. The international community stood on the brink of a transformative moment, united by a common goal and the unwavering belief that through diplomacy, collaboration, and collective action, they could shape a better future for the world's children.

Amid the bustling preparations and diplomatic intricacies, a poignant reminder of the true impact of the resolution resonated in the hearts of those involved who were survivors. These were the individuals whose lives had been shaped by the very issues the resolution sought to address: from those who were abused by a member of their circle of trust, to those trafficked by cartels and those who were exploited online. Finally, their voices would be heard through this resolution.

The survivors' stories, each a testament to resilience and strength, served as a driving force for all. The world day for children presented them a beacon of hope, a promise of a future where survivors' voices were no longer silent, and where they no longer suffered in shame.

As the sun set on November 6th, a sense of purposeful serenity settled over the Assembly Hall. The stage was set, the Missions were ready, and the resolution's journey was about to take its most profound step yet, with the possibilities far beyond the walls of the United Nations and into the annals of history of the child protection movement.

Jenny knew everyone had done their best, and now it was time to wait, and pray.

8

THE SUN WAS JUST PEAKING over the horizon when Jenny awoke the morning of the big day. She looked out the window, and overnight the leaves of the trees had turned a golden brown, and the air had grown fresh and crisp. She dressed in a red suit, put on black patent leather shoes, and packed her backpack for the day. She called her friend Sara, and they ate breakfast and made their way to the Mission.

When they arrived, they were greeted by the warm smiles of the Ambassador and his staff. Ms. Finda joined them, and all were stunned when she shared the news that over 80 UN member states had signed on to sponsor the resolution. There was a profound sense of excitement and anticipation in the air, as it seemed hopeful that the vote would pass.

Then Fatima arrived. She had a presence that commanded both attention and respect. When their eyes met, Jenny saw a reflection of her own resilience, a mirror to the strength she had discovered within herself. It was a silent affirmation that their paths had converged for a reason, that their stories had intertwined to create a force more significant than the sum of their parts.

Fatima invited Jenny to accompany her delegation, and they drove together with Ambassador Turay to the ground-floor entrance of the General Assembly building. When they exited the car, the other members of Fatima's delegation were waiting at the entrance to greet them. They walked through the doors, each reflecting on the journey that had brought them to this point. No matter what happened, they knew they had done their best.

The survivors sat together in the public gallery of the main Assembly room. As they waited patiently for the resolution to be tabled, they made new friends and formed alliances that would last for decades to come. Amid the diplomatic formalities and official proceedings, the presence of the survivors was palpable. As the Plenary session commenced, it was not only the nations and diplomats who were represented – it was the survivors' aspirations and dreams that were given voice and purpose.

Jenny entered the General Assembly Hall with Fatima holding her hand. She was captivated by the buzz of languages from all corners of the globe. The unity in diversity was striking, as diplomats dressed in their nations' traditional attire sat side by side, fostering a sense of harmony despite their unique opinions and differences. Jenny felt humbled in the presence of such great men and women, and deeply honored to be invited to join them on the floor of the Assembly.

As they waited for the resolution to be tabled, Jenny admired the beautiful architecture of the great hall. It was a masterpiece of elegant lines, curves, and angles, meticulously designed to foster openness and collaboration among the foreign leaders and diplomats gathered within.

At the center of the hall was a grand podium where world leaders and diplomats addressed their positions to the global audience. Its polished wood matched the rich paneling of the walls surrounding the stage, reflecting the earnest dedication poured into shaping the destinies of nations. Behind it, an enormous backdrop bared an emblem – a circle of olive branches encircling the world map. It was a poignant reminder of the United Nations' mission to promote global peace and cooperation.

The room grew quiet when it was time for the General Assembly to consider the world day resolution. The anticipation in the air was palpable, as twenty additional Member States had agreed to sponsor the resolution, bringing the total number to 100. Then, Fatima got up and walked to the great podium. With each step, the excitement of the delegation and the survivor community grew. All had great hopes that she would convince the world's leaders to vote yes.

When she arrived at the podium, Fatima stood for a moment; her eyes sparkled in the glow of the golden light that shone on the stage as she gazed into the audience. Jenny remembered the magical moment they had first met under the great Juniper Tree, and she heard Fatima's beautiful song of love and compassion for the world's children. This fairy tale was coming to life before her eyes.

All grew silent, and Jenny and her friends held their breath, wondering what Fatima might say to the Great Assembly. Then she began her speech.

The Ambassadors and leaders of the world listened as Fatima spoke with passion and reverence about the need to protect children. She told of the great hardships those who had lost their dignity had faced. She asked for help to bring those who harmed children to justice and to support the healing of all the children of the world that had been harmed.

Everyone stood and clapped when Fatima concluded her speech. She returned to her seat with the delegation, and all was silent again. Then His Excellency António Manuel de Oliveira Guterres, the Secretary General of the United Nations, read the declaration, and he asked if any other Member States wished to sponsor the resolution. An additional 18 nations pressed their buttons, bringing the number to an impressive 118.

It was a historic moment, and Fatima and Jenny cried as Ambassador Guterres read the list of Member States who agreed to sponsor the resolution. Then, His Excellency Guterres called for the vote, and the Members of the General Assembly voted unanimously to declare the 18th of November as a day of observance to protect the dignity of the world's children and help survivors of abuse in their healing journey.

After the vote, everyone cheered, and all those present came to congratulate Fatima, the Ambassadors, and the staff of the Missions of Sierra Leone and Nigeria, and all those at the UN and beyond who had worked hard on the resolution. Jenny felt a deep sense of satisfaction. The world's leaders had recognized the value of children and made a commitment to implement policies to protect their dignity and help victims of abuse to restore their lives.

Although a great deal had been accomplished, it was just the beginning. But it was an auspicious beginning with great promise.

The following week, Fatima, Jenny, and their friends and survivors of child abuse from around the world flew to Rome, Italy, to commemorate the first world day at the Vatican. They met with Pope Francis, the Holy See, and he blessed them and asked God to support them and all the brave men and women worldwide who worked so diligently each day to protect the children.

Then Fatima, Jenny, and their friends said their goodbyes and parted ways. Jenny's heart felt both heavy and light, a paradoxical blend of feelings that mirrored the complexity of the human experience. She understood that this moment marked the closing of a chapter, but also the beginning of new journeys for each of them.

It was a bittersweet moment as Jenny watched her friends walk away, the echoes of their laughter and shared experiences etched in her memory, each taking with them the cherished moments and the special bonds they had forged, knowing their paths might cross again in the tapestry of life.

As Jenny stood in St. Peter's Square, a mixture of emotions swirled within her. She had a deep sense of gratitude for the growth and healing she had experienced alongside so many extraordinary individuals. Before leaving Rome, she visited the Basilica of San Giovanni in Laterano. She placed 100 euros in the offering box, and she lit candles in gratitude for all those who had supported her on her remarkable journey.

She prayed for the healing of survivors of abuse around the world. She gave thanks for President Tinubu and his delegation for their collaboration and co-facilitation, for the organizations who advocated for and supported the world day, and for the many leaders and staff at the United Nations who helped craft the resolution. Finally, she gave thanks for the great gift the President and First Lady and the Mission of the Republic of Sierra Leone had given to them all.

As Jenny flew home, her plane crossed the Arctic circle, and they were treated to a spectacular light show called the aurora borealis. All peered out the windows in awe as vibrant ribbons of green, pink, and purple danced across the stars. It was a transcendent moment, where the vastness of the universe met the collective wonder of its spectators.

Each pulse of color, every shimmering wave, whispered tales of ancient mysteries and cosmic wonders. As the auroras continued their ballet, the cabin was filled with hushed reverence, a shared experience of witnessing nature's most ethereal masterpiece. For Jenny, it was a gentle reminder of the world's boundless beauty and the magic that awaited in unexpected moments.

10

When Jenny returned to Cambridge, she visited the great juniper tree once again. She was grateful that the world's leaders promised to work harder to protect children, but deep inside her soul, there was a force lurking in the shadows that threatened to rob her of her joy. She touched the branch of the great tree, hoping it might heal the deep wounds that continued to haunt her dreams.

"Great spirit, can you share your wisdom with me?" she asked. She closed her eyes, and the spirit of the tree embraced her, and then she heard the whisper of Fatima's song in the distance. When she opened her eyes, she saw a beautiful angel; its magnificent light infusing all the living things she could see. The angel shared the wisdom of the great spirit with Jenny:

"There will always be suffering in the world. Do not let the darkness of the deeds of those who dance in the shadows of misery destroy your soul. Let go of the pain they have caused you to make room for the light. Only then can you truly embrace the beauty that life has to offer."

"As you walk the path of forgiveness, you will not erase the wrongs done to you, nor will you condone the actions of those who cause you pain. Rather, you will release the chains that tie you to the past, allowing you to heal. Just as the great juniper tree needs tending to flourish, your heart requires the nurturing of forgiveness to bloom anew. Letting go will not diminish you or the gravity of what occurred; it will set you free."

In this, Jenny came to understand that forgiveness was a powerful and liberating choice. As time passed, she decided to forgive the boys who hurt her so long ago. She knew her forgiveness did not excuse their actions, but her decision meant they no longer had the power to rob her of her happiness.

For Jenny, the juniper tree had come to symbolize the timeless bonds of friendship, the enduring power of nature, the resilience of the human spirit, the essence of compassion and empathy, and the boundless potential of our dreams.

When Jenny returned home from her visit to the juniper tree, she saw the *Grimms' Fairy Tales* book resting on her coffee table. She opened the book and began reading where she had left off when she was in the Harvard Coop bookstore what seemed like a lifetime ago.

The stories in the beautiful book came alive again, transporting her to the realms of imagination and wonder. The characters and their adventures welcomed her as if no time had passed since she last journeyed alongside them, weaving her through a journey of emotions, from exhilarating highs to heart-wrenching lows, mirroring the spectrum of the human experience.

The triumphs and setbacks of the characters in the centuries-old stories resonated with Jenny's journey and the journeys of countless others who had walked the path of life. The more she immersed herself in the tales of courage, love, loss, and resilience, the more she recognized the timeless nature of human struggles and aspirations.

As she turned to the book's last page, she realized how much she had learned and grown since coming to Harvard. How the past spoke to the present, offering insight and solace, and how the human spirit's capacity to overcome adversity transcended eras and generations. She learned the value of character and virtue, and the promise of forgiveness.

She learned that her fears, doubts, and insecurities were not unique to her alone but were threads woven into the fabric of every individual's life, and that authenticity was a source of connection rather than weakness.

Jenny thought about Fatima and Julius and their devotion to improving the lives of women and children in Sierra Leone. They faced immense challenges as they struggled to uplift a country ravaged by civil war and poverty, yet they took time to answer the call of survivors of abuse a world away, whose voices had been ignored for too long.

She thought of the journey they had all embarked on together that would spark a global movement, and she felt an overwhelming sense of pride and gratitude. She hoped the story of their meeting, and the magical events that transpired might help other survivors reclaim their voices, and transform their narrative, as it had transformed hers.

And so, the legend of Fatima and the Juniper Tree spread far and wide, inspiring leaders across the world to plant and nurture seeds of hope with actions in their nations that might protect children and bring healing to the wounded hearts of those who lost their dignity, so all may flourish.

THE END

Epilogue
True Story of the 18 November World Day

When a story involves the abuse of a child, it has the power to stir strong emotions like anger, sadness, empathy, and fear. There is a natural response for people to instinctively shy away from such topics, to shield themselves from the distressing feelings that can arise. Fatima and the Juniper Tree therefore approaches the topic through folklore to allow readers to explore the issue of child abuse and process their emotions from a safe distance, while recognizing the importance of addressing this challenging issue.

Through story and fairy tales, folklore imparts valuable lessons, wisdom, and knowledge to our society. By leveraging the power of imagination, symbolism, and cultural context, folklore creates a bridge between the abstract and the concrete, providing a sense of connection, empathy, and reflection without overwhelming the reader or listener with the raw intensity of the subject matter.

Among the most notable of folklore tales are the stories of the 19th century German authors, the Grimm Brothers. Their collection of fairy tales is an amalgamation of stories originating from Scandinavia, Spain, the Netherlands, Ireland, Scotland, England, Serbia, and Finland. First published in 1812, their narratives contain moral teachings, practical advice, and insights into human behavior, all designed to guide readers through life's challenges. *The Juniper Tree* is one of the darkest tales in Grimms' collection. It shares the story of a young boy who is killed by his stepmother, and unknowingly fed to his father. His bones are collected and buried beneath a juniper tree by his dog. The boy's soul emerges as a bird who sings about his murder, and he is thus avenged. He then returns to life with the aid of the tree.

MY JOURNEY

When I began my journey to establish a World Day for survivors of abuse, I had no idea that Harvard would help bring my dream to fruition. It served as a unique convening force that allowed me to overcome many barriers and break through obstacles to achieve results that seemed miraculous at times. It was a true fairy tale.

On a rainy day in March of 2020, I met Dr. Katelyn Long, the John and Daria Barry post-doctoral fellow at the Human Flourishing Program at Harvard University and a postdoctoral fellow at the Harvard T.H. Chan School of Public Health. We sat at a café in Harvard Square and talked over a cup of tea and nibbled on chocolate croissants. Although we had very different backgrounds, we shared many of the same interests in religion, spirituality, and health.

We talked about my first book, *A Letter to the Pope*, which addressed my family's experience following the discovery of both my brothers having been abused at the hands of our beloved parish priest. She was intrigued with my personal journey, my experiences with the Church, and my emerging research on forgiveness. As we talked about our backgrounds and aspirations, I shared my dream of coming to Harvard to do research and hopefully teach one day.

A few weeks after our meeting in Cambridge, Kate introduced me to Dr. Tyler VanderWeele, the John L. Loeb and Frances Lehman Loeb Professor of Epidemiology in the Departments of Epidemiology and Biostatistics at the Harvard T.H. Chan School of Public Health. Among his many distinctions, Tyler serves as the co-founder and Director of Harvard's Human Flourishing Program (HFH) and as the Co-Director of the Initiative on Health, Religion and Spirituality.

Tyler agreed to talk with me, where we discussed my background and research interests, and he invited me to submit a proposal. A few months later, I was offered an appointment as a Research Associate within The Faculty of Arts and Sciences, and I was invited to join the Human Flourishing Program research team.

In the fall of 2020, amidst the COVID pandemic, I put my belongings into a storage unit, packed a suitcase, and loaded it along with several boxes of essentials into my car. It was filled to the brim, but there was just enough room in the front seat for a little bed for my constant companion and fearless therapy dog, Jasper, a precocious Maltese with a smile that would melt any heart. Together we drove 3,200 miles to Boston, where I embarked on the journey of a lifetime.

When I arrived, Harvard's campus had just closed due to the pandemic, so I spent much of the year alone in my loft, zooming into meetings and conducting my research online. I got to know my colleagues through a Monday morning weekly call where we would check in with one another, talk about developments, and share stories on how we were coping with the pandemic. During one of our program's weekly chat sessions, my colleague, Dr. Matthew (Matt) Lee, shared that he would be teaching a course on social justice and was looking for projects that he might assign to his students that they could work on virtually.

In hopeful anticipation of getting some support for the World Day, I shared my work on this idea with Matt, and he and several students jumped in to help. Then Tyler agreed to sponsor a symposium to foster faith and flourishing for victims of child sexual abuse. With the help of Dr. Brendan Case, Associate Director of Research for the HFH program, the symposium was a huge success. We brought together 73 speakers from 23 countries, including subject matter experts and world-renowned leaders in the field of child abuse prevention from the UN, UNICEF, WHO, USAID, World Vision, academia, commissions, religious organizations, child advocacy organizations, and child sexual abuse survivors.

The keynote address for our symposium was delivered by Dr. Dennis Mukwege, the 2018 Peace Prize Nobel Laureat. Over 1,500 individuals participated from more than 40 countries over three days of virtual presentations and roundtable discussions. The program received the blessing of all the major houses of worship, including an address by His Holiness Pope

Francis during the General Assembly, a blessing by Cardinal Sean O'Malley, and a message from Queen Sylvia of Sweden.

For me, the symposium illustrated the unique power of Harvard's convening force. We brought together diverse faith traditions, academic institutions, public health practitioners, world leaders, and survivors to begin to tackle one of the world's most daunting and intractable human problems. We created a safe place for all to come together to share, listen, and learn. It provided me with an opportunity to gain a deeper perspective of the global religious and political landscape and the role faith leaders play in shaping views and influencing cultural practices in various societies around the globe.

Following the symposium, we formed the Global Collaborative, a network of NGO's, governmental agencies, survivor networks,, and academic institutions, led by survivors that came together to advocate for the World Day. Over 50 organizations signed an open letter to world leaders to request action. With this letter in hand, we approached ambassadors and diplomats around the world, hoping to find a nation that might sponsor the day.

We were advised that a World Day was an impossible dream, and one by one, we were turned down. I almost gave up hope, until I met with Her Excellency, Fatima Maada Bio, the First Lady of the Republic of Sierra Leone. When she learned of our dream to establish a World Day, she offered to help us. When I shared that we needed a UN member state to launch the initiative, she said six words that forever changed my world. "You must meet with my husband." I met His Excellency, President Julius Maada Bio during his state visit to Washington DC, in September of 2021, and the rest is history. I hope you enjoyed our story.

CHILD SEXUAL ABUSE AND EXPLOITATION (CSAE)

CSAE is a grave violation of human rights and is among the most significant violations of dignity a person can experience. It is not solely restricted to physical contact; such abuse could include noncontact abuse, such as exposure, voyeurism, and child pornography.

The World Health Organization reports 120 million girls and young women under 20 years of age have suffered some form of forced sexual contact; that one in five women, and one in thirteen men report experiencing sexual abuse before their 18th birthday; and that in some parts of the world, one out of every two children has experienced sexual abuse; and that because of the shame, stigma, and fear associated with their experience, at least sixty percent of child sexual abuse victims/survivors never disclose their abuse.

Despite the widespread view that most children who experience sexual abuse are assaulted by strangers, many children are abused by someone in their circle of trust, such as a member of the child's immediate family, a friend or relative of the family, or someone whom the child encounters on a regular basis (childcare worker, coach, teacher, camp counselor, priest or pastor, or health care provider).

As a result of the COVID-19 pandemic, extreme poverty, hunger, unemployment, inequality, and violence are rising. Tragically, the necessary measures taken to mitigate the spread of COVID-19 have placed many children at greater risk of experiencing child marriage, trafficking, and sexual violence, abuse, and exploitation, both online and offline.

The ramifications of CSAE often extend into adulthood and can lead to adverse effects on one's mental and physical health, as well as on their economic independence by destroying their opportunity to achieve their full potential. If victims do not get the help they need to heal, many will likely live anguished lives.

The statistics on child sexual abuse and its consequences constitute a public health crisis. Public health and welfare agencies have a key role in preventing CSAE, by identifying and providing care and supportive services to victims of CSAE. However, many do not have access to the resources required to address these challenges. Several factors contribute to the struggle to address this critical concern:

1. **Underreporting**: Child sexual abuse often goes unreported due to factors like fear, shame, and the child's vulnerability. This makes it difficult for authorities to accurately assess the scope of the problem and allocate resources effectively.
2. **Stigma and Shame**: Societal stigma associated with child sexual abuse can discourage victims, families, and communities from openly discussing or reporting incidents. This stigma can hinder awareness campaigns and the creation of safe spaces for victims to seek help.
3. **Complex Legal Processes**: Prosecuting child sexual abuse cases can be challenging due to the legal complexities involved, including the need to protect victims while gathering evidence and ensuring due process for the accused.
4. **Cross-border and Online Challenges**: The globalization of information and technology has led to cases of child sexual abuse crossing international borders and occurring in online spaces. This presents jurisdictional challenges and requires cooperation between countries to address effectively.
5. **Resource Constraints**: Addressing child sexual abuse requires a significant allocation of resources, including funding for prevention, intervention, support services, and law enforcement efforts. Many governments may struggle to allocate sufficient resources given competing priorities.

6. **Lack of Coordination**: Effective response to child sexual abuse requires collaboration among various sectors, including law enforcement, social services, healthcare, education, and NGOs. Lack of coordination between these entities can hinder progress.
7. **Child Protection Systems**: Strengthening child protection systems involves policy development, training for professionals, and public education. Governments may face hurdles in implementing and monitoring these systems consistently.
8. **Cultural and Social Factors**: Cultural norms and societal attitudes can influence how child sexual abuse is perceived and addressed. Some societies may be resistant to acknowledging the issue due to cultural taboos or misconceptions.
9. **Prevention and Education**: Implementing effective prevention programs and educational initiatives requires a sustained effort to change attitudes, behaviors, and norms. This demands continuous investment and long-term commitment.
10. **Trauma-Informed Care**: Providing appropriate support and care for child sexual abuse survivors requires a trauma-informed approach. Training professionals to recognize and respond to trauma can be a complex undertaking.

To address child sexual abuse effectively, governments need to prioritize comprehensive strategies that encompass prevention, intervention, support services, legal reforms, awareness campaigns, and international collaboration. Overcoming these challenges requires a collective effort involving policymakers, law enforcement, healthcare providers, educators, social workers, and the broader community to ensure the safety and well-being of children.

The Council of Europe on the Convention on Protection of Children against Sexual Exploitation and Sexual Abuse, also known as "the Lanzarote Convention," provides a forum for nations to come together to address the issue of child sexual abuse. The Convention set up specific legislation nations may adopt and measures they can take to prevent sexual violence, to protect child victims, and to prosecute perpetrators. It is my goal and hope that this book can contribute to furthering awareness and actions in all these critical areas.

For more information on the topic of child sexual abuse, and recommendations for policies and programs you can implement to keep children safe and support survivors, please visit Global Collaborative at **globalcollaborative.org**.

General Assembly

Seventy-seventh session
Agenda item

Resolution by the 77th General Assembly on 7 November 2022

[on the recommendation of the Third Committee]

World Day for the Prevention of, and Healing from Child Sexual Exploitation, Abuse and Violence

The General Assembly,

Guided by the purposes and principles of the Charter of the United Nations,

Recalling its resolutions 53/199 of 15 December 1998 and 61/185 of 20 December 2006 on the proclamation of international years and Economic and Social Council resolution 1980/67 of 25 July 1980 on international years and anniversaries,

Reaffirming the Universal Declaration of Human Rights,[1] the Convention on the Rights of the Child[2] as well as its Optional Protocols,[3] International Covenant on Economic, Social, and Cultural Rights,[4] the International Covenant on Civil and Political Rights,[5] the Convention against Transnational Organized Crime, and recalling all other relevant international treaties,

Recalling that the 2030 Agenda for Sustainable Development places the dignity of children and their right to live free from violence as a priority on the international development agenda through the implementation of the range of goals and targets of the 2030 Agenda for Sustainable Development relevant to ending exploitation, abuse, trafficking, torture and all forms of violence against children, as well as eliminating all harmful practices, such as child, early and forced marriage, and female genital mutilation, which place children at risk of experiencing child sexual exploitation, abuse and violence,

Expressing grave concern that children especially girls are at a greater risk of experiencing forced sex, sexual exploitation, abuse and violence, including both online and offline, in particular during armed conflict and that because of the shame, stigma, and fear associated with their experiences, many victims and survivors never disclose and/or seek justice, rehabilitation or support, and that many victims and survivors of child abuse experience lifelong consequences to their physical and mental health and wellbeing,

Affirming the need to eliminate and prevent all forms of child sexual exploitation, abuse, and violence and to promote the dignity, rights, including mental and physical health and healing for those who experience childhood sexual exploitation, abuse, and violence,

1. *Decides* to proclaim 18 November each year as the World Day for the Prevention of and Healing from Child Sexual Exploitation, Abuse and Violence.

2. *Invites* all Member States, relevant organizations of the United Nations system and other international organizations, world leaders, and faith actors, civil society, including non-governmental organizations, academic institutions, as well as the private sector, and other relevant stakeholders, to commemorate the World Day for the Prevention of and Healing from Child Sexual Exploitation, Abuse and Violence each year in a manner that each considers most appropriate, including through commitments to ensure quality education, and to raise public awareness of those impacted by Sexual child abuse and the need to prevent and eliminate child sexual exploitation, abuse, and violence including online and offline, and the imperative to hold perpetrators to account, and ensure the access of survivors and victims' to justice and remedies, as well as facilitate open discussion on the need to prevent and eliminate their stigmatization, promote their healing, affirm their dignity, and protect their rights.

3. *Stresses* that the cost of all activities that may arise from the implementation of the present resolution shall be met from voluntary contributions.

4. *Requests* the Secretary-General to bring the present resolution to the attention of all Member States and United Nations Systems.

His Excellency, Julius Maada Bio, President of the Republic of Sierra Leone and Her Excellency, Fatima Maada Bio, the First Lady

Acknowledgments

The World Day would not have been possible without the support and encouragement of the survivor community, and the co-founders of the Global Collaborative: Michael Hoffman, Mark Williams, Sara Dekker, Susie Greco, and Nadia Jamil who stood by me throughout this incredible journey.

We are forever indebted to Melissa Merrick, President of Prevent Child Abuse of America for serving as the founding partner of our collaborative.

I am grateful to Dr. Tyler VanderWeele and my colleagues at the Human Flourishing Program at Harvard University for their encouragement and support, and to Dr. David Holland, at Harvard Divinity School for his partnership, and taking the journey to Rome to help commemorate the first World Day with us.

Along the way, we had the support of many individuals and organizations who committed time and resources to help us fulfill our dream. I am especially grateful to Nicole Epps, former Executive Director of the World Childhood Foundation, for standing by me through many trials and tribulations.

We are forever grateful to Nicole and the World Childhood Foundation for sponsoring our first UN side-event in July of 2021. I am also grateful to May Hassoon, Executive Advisor and to Anwar Khan, President of Islamic Relief, USA for their advocacy and support of our cause.

We thank The Catholic Project and The Catholic University of America for sponsoring our symposium and supporting the many events and activities we hosted to advance the World Day in the faith community and beyond. I thank Hans Zolner, S.J., for his lifelong commitment to protecting children, for his guidance and support of our symposium, for the beautiful Mass held at the Vatican in honor of the first World Day, and for being a man of honor, and a cherished friend.

I am grateful for His Excellency, Cardinal Sean O'Malley, President of the Pontifical Commission for the Protection of Minors, and its members and staff, including Father Andrew Small, for accompanying us on our journey and supporting our work on a global scale, both within the Catholic Church and beyond. I thank His Excellency, Cardinal Joseph Tobin for walking with us in Baltimore in honor of the first "unofficial" World Day on November 18, 2022, and His Excellency, Cardinal Blase Cupich for arranging an audience for our delegation with His Holiness during our visit to Rome to commemorate the first official World Day. I thank His Excellency, Archbishop Gabrielle Caccia and his staff for their support and guidance on the world day resolution.

Finally, I thank the leadership and staff of the many organizations that supported us along our journey:

A Breeze of Hope Foundation
American Professional Society on the Abuse of Children
Arigatou International
Army of Survivors
Australia eSafety Commission
Advocates for Women's and Kids' Equality (AWAKE)
Berkley Center for Religion, Peace, and World Affairs
Bellweather International
Candle In A Dark Room
Child Abuse Council
Christian Cultural Center
Darkness to Light
Global Partnership to End Violence Against Children
General Federation of Women's Clubs (GFWC)
End Child Prostitution in Asian Tourism (ECPAT)
End FGM/C U.S./Network
Enough Abuse Campaign
Foundations and Donors Interested in Catholic Activities (FADICA)
Hands Off Our Girls
Human Flourishing Program, Harvard University
Interfaith Alliance for Safer Communities
International Board of Rabbis
International Society for the Prevention of Child Abuse & Neglect (ISPCAN)
Keep Kids Safe Coalition
Islamic Relief
Male Survivors
Maria Goretti Network
Monique Burr Foundation
National Center on Sexual Exploitation
New York Board of Rabbis
Program of All-Inclusive Care for the Elderly (PACE)
Prevent Child Abuse America
Reaching All HIV+ Muslims in America (RAHMA)
Roads of Success
Sacred Spaces
Shine on Sierra Leone
Survivor Network for those Abused by Priests (SNAP)
The Catholic Project
The National Foundation to End Child Abuse and Neglect (EndCAN)
The New York Foundling
Their Story is Our Story
WeProtect Global Alliance
World Childhood Foundation, USA
World Council of Churches
World Vision
YMCA USA

About the Author

Jennifer S. Wortham, Dr.PH, is a religion, spirituality, and forgiveness research associate at the Human Flourishing Program at Harvard University, and Associate Research Professor at Claremont Graduate University. She earned her doctorate in public health at UCLA Fielding School of Public Health, where she teaches graduate-level courses in health services quality improvement and Lean management practices. She has extensive experience in health system transformation, and has served as a strategy and quality improvement consultant for leading healthcare organizations in the public and private sectors for over 30 years.

Dr. Wortham's current research focuses on the impact of moral and spiritual injury on health outcomes. She is leading research on the development of psycho-social-spiritual interventions for victims of traumatic life events and moral injury. In 2018, she authored a memoir on forgiveness titled *A Letter to the Pope: The Keeper of the Nest*, based on her family's experience with clergy abuse. In 2023, she co-authored *Moral Injury: A Handbook for Military Chaplains.*

Dr. Wortham chairs the Global Collaborative, an initiative of the Solace Institute focused on promoting awareness of child abuse and advocating for support for survivors through the November 18 World Day.

Please join us in recognizing the 18 November World Day for the Prevention of, and Healing from Child Sexual Exploitation, Abuse and Violence.

KEY ACTIONS GOVERNMENTS AND CIVIL SOCIETY CAN TAKE

1. **Visit the Lanzarote Convention** online at coe.int/en/web/children/convention.

2. **Establish a proclamation in support** of the 18 November World Day.

3. **Host special events and forums** for victims and survivors of abuse to elevate their voices and gain a deeper understanding of the issue from those with lived experience.

4. **Allocate funding for child protection**, sexual abuse prevention, criminal justice systems, restorative justice, and health and welfare agencies.

5. **Learn the steps all people can take** to prevent child sexual abuse by visiting globalcollaborative.org online.

BOOK GROUP AND CLASS DISCUSSION QUESTIONS

Following are questions for book clubs and classrooms:

1. What did you like about this book?

2. What did you not like about this book?

3. Was there any one line or passage that stood out to you?

4. Does this book remind you of any other books?

5. What feelings or emotions does this book evoke in you?

6. What was the author's purpose in writing this book?

7. What ideas was she trying to get across?

8. How original and unique was this book?

9. If there were any twists or reveals, how believable were they?

10. What messages do you think the author was trying to convey through various forms of symbolism in the book?

NOTES

Made in the USA
Columbia, SC
29 August 2023